SERIOUS
APPLICANTS
ONLY

Also by Aric Sundquist

SERIOUS APPLICANTS ONLY

A Horror Comedy
by
Aric Sundquist

Dark Peninsula Press LLC

Table of Contents

Author's Note:

This story uses endnotes indicated by lowercase Roman numerals. Feel free to read them however you wish—during the story or after (they are listed on page 91). This revised paperback version also includes a bonus short story at the end. Enjoy!

SERIOUS
APPLICANTS
ONLY

Chapter 1

Mary Sanderson stood in front of a plain brick building at the end of a vacant street. No signs were visible outside the structure, not even a parking lot. Instead, only a plain white building with a gigantic steel door thick enough to resist a charging tank.

She knocked on the door. No response. She tried again, louder this time. Still nothing. Confused, she opened her purse and pulled out a sheet of paper printed from a job posting on the internet.

Wanted: Experienced safety supervisor to work in an experimental weapons facility. Must have a practical mind, look ravishing in a lab coat, and be willing to use a flamethrower if things take a turn for the worse.

Serious applicants only, please.

There was no way the advertisement could be real. More than once she wondered if the ad was a practical joke—perhaps a sorority prank or a hidden camera TV show. Guess there was only one way to find out.

Mary rapped on the door again, as hard as she could, and then noticed a speaker imbedded near the doorway. It looked like an outdated intercom system. She leaned over, pushed the button and said quietly, "Hello?"

A voice answered through the intercom speaker. "Hello. What can I do for you?"

"Yes, my name is Mary Sanderson. I'm here for a job interview. I was emailed by Mr. Ashford and told to come to this address at nine a.m. today."

"Ah, yes!" the voice said. "Mary... that's right! I'm Mr. Ashford! But call me Owen. You'll have to wait a minute, however. The whole facility is on lock down at the moment."

"Lock down? For what?"

"We had an accident with one of our experiments. Nothing to worry about, really. Out of curiosity, do you know anything about wormholes?"

"Wormholes? A little, I guess. What do you want to know?"

"How to stop them."

"Stop them from what?"

"From getting bigger."

"For real?"

"I'm afraid so. The staff ended up opening a portal to another dimension. From what they've been saying, it's getting bigger and bigger every second. But don't worry. I mean… how big can a wormhole get?" He laughed.

"Actually, they can get pretty big."

"Really? How big?"

"They can swallow whole planets and solar systems."

Silence.

"Hello?" Mary said, leaning closer to the speaker.

"Yes, well… we might have a more urgent problem than I had previously anticipated. We can still do the interview, but things might be a bit more hectic around here than normal. What do you say—are you still up for it?"

"Sure, I guess."

"That's the spirit. Please enter."

The door unlocked.

Mary pushed open the door but didn't dare enter. Instead, she peered cautiously into the darkness.

Within moments, a man in his sixties stood before her, holding a folded lab coat. He regarded her with bushy white eyebrows that reminded her of frost in January. He had a genuine smile.

"Try this on," he said, handing over the folded coat.

Mary took the jacket and slipped it on over her black blouse and skirt. The lab coat fit nice and snug and was clean smelling, with just a faint trace of bleach. She always liked that smell, for some reason.

"It looks good on you," he said. "By the way, have you ever fired a gun?"

"What does that have to do with anything?"

"I suppose I'm getting ahead of myself. Would you please follow me to my office? I'll explain everything shortly."

She entered the building and followed Owen down the hall and into a brightly lit office. He sat down in front of his desk. It contained stacks of papers and a desktop computer.

"Have a seat," he said, motioning to the chair.

Mary sat on a black leather chair. "Is this ad serious," she asked, placing it on the table and sliding it over.

"Yes, quite serious," he said. "Although the lab coat part was a bit of a joke from the techs. They're a little sexist, I'm afraid, but mostly harmless. Do you have experience with CPR and basic first aid?"

"Yes, I do. I have a degree in respiratory therapy, and I worked as an EMT for three years. But nothing to do with weapons."

"What was your GPA in college?"

"3.8."

"And why aren't you pursuing a job as a respiratory therapist?"

"I didn't like it."

"Why not?"

"I didn't like being around people who were dying all the time, especially newborns. In college, they don't teach you how to deal with that kind of thing. So I started getting depressed, and I had trouble sleeping at night, which led to a drinking problem. Eventually I knew I couldn't do it anymore, so I quit, along with the drinking. The EMT gig was long hours and bad pay, so that's why I'm here."

"I like your answers. They're honest."

"Thank you."

Owen was about to ask another question when the intercom system beeped and flashed red. "Excuse me a second," he said.

"No problem."

He answered the call. "What is it? I'm in the middle of an interview."

"Phillip's gone!" a man yelled through the speaker. "He got sucked into that stupid wormhole!"

"Wait a minute. Is this Nicholas again?"

"Yes!"

"Okay, Nick... I'm not a scientist, remember? Why are you telling me this?"

"I don't know! I didn't know who else to call!"

"Okay, just calm down and tell me what happened."

"Okay, well—we were staring into that wormhole, you know, and contemplating all that stuff you're supposed to contemplate while staring into something dark and infinite. Then Phil started throwing rocks inside it. He said he wanted to see how deep it went. And then next thing we knew... he hit something on the head, and it came slithering out and grabbed him!"

"What was it that grabbed him?"

"I don't know! I wasn't there!"

"Then how do you know something grabbed him?"

"Because there's a trail of slime leading from the wormhole all the way down to his lab! And now he's missing! What should I do?"

"Okay, first find a priest and get him to bless you."

"I'm Jewish, but okay... I will!"

"Second, you should go in after him."

"Inside the wormhole? Are you crazy! It's too deep! We couldn't even hear the rocks landing!"

"Okay, then find a ladder."

"A ladder won't help! We need something a lot longer than that!"

"Then get two ladders and tape them together. Jesus man, do I have to think of everything?"

"Wait a minute... you're just messing with me, aren't you?"

"A little. I have to go. Like I said, I'm interviewing someone."

"Wait a minute... are you interviewing someone for the safety supervisor position?"

"Yes."

"A woman?"

"Yes."

"Is she hot?"

"She's a very attractive young woman."

"Sweet! I got dibs! Talk to you later!"

The line went dead.

Owen hung up his phone. "My apologies, Mary. And don't worry—he won't jump inside that wormhole. He doesn't have the spine for it."

"What the fuck's going on here?" she asked. "This can't be serious. There's a hidden camera around here somewhere, right?"

"I assure you, this is all very serious. The men working here create weapons beyond our wildest imagination. But when it comes to menial tasks... for instance, mowing the lawn, or cooking dinner, or NOT saying out loud a deadly curse found on an ancient sarcophagus, well... they just flat out fail. That's where you come in. We need someone with a little common sense around here. Your medical training will come in handy, too, for obvious reasons. Now tell me—have you ever fired a gun a before?"

"Actually, yes. My dad is a former Navy Seal. Growing up, he'd take me out to his father's hunting cabin in Minnesota, and we'd take turns shooting tin cans with his Sig Saur."

"Splendid. You're hired."

"But Owen, I don't think I'm qualified for this job. It seems too weird for me. I'm not sure if this is fake or—"

"Does three grand a week sound good?"

Mary's tongue got tied up. She wanted to say *no*, but couldn't. She needed the money, desperately. College is damned expensive.

"When do you want me to start?" she asked.

"Right now."

Chapter 2

Owen presented Mary with a stack of forms requiring her signature. She signed and dated each one. One of the forms stated that the Halcyon Weapons Corporation would not be held liable in the case of an accidental death within the facility. Although Mary wasn't comfortable signing a non-liability agreement, especially with a company that specialized in experimental weapons, he assured her that the insurance payout was too high to consider suing anyway. She ended up signing on the dotted line.

"Now for stage two," he said, filing the papers away. "You have two hours to complete a written placement exam." He slid over the test along with a #2 pencil and gave her a big smile.

"Seriously?" she asked. "Is this maybe something I should study for?"

"Not really. It's more about how you'll fit in with the company. Don't worry, you'll be fine."

"And a #2 pencil? That seems..."

"Outdated?"

"Yes."

"Everything in this facility is outdated. It's best not to question it and just try to manage the best you can."

Mary nodded. She picked up the exam and began reading the first page.

Question #1: Please tell us your religious affiliation in one sentence or less.

Question #2: In the case of demonic possession, is the above religion your chosen form of protection?

Question #3: If you answered "yes" to the above question, please skip to question #4. If you answered "no," please elaborate upon your religious confusion in one paragraph or less.

Question #4: If an alien lifeform cloned your body, tell us in one paragraph the best way to identify yourself from your clone.

Question #5: To further identify yourself from alien cloning, answer "yes" if you would like to have a safe word on file that will secretly inform any non-cloned survivors that you are indeed a non-cloned survivor. If you choose to not have a safe word on file, please answer "no" and proceed to question #7, but please be aware that you may be subject to a random DNA test at any given time during your employment with HWC.

Question #6: If you answered "yes" to the above question, please supply your personal safe word in the space provided.

Question #7: If you were in the desert and saw a tortoise flipped over on its back and struggling in the hot sun, would you flip it over, or would you leave it alone and let nature run its course?

Mary stuck her head down and started filling in the questions to the best of her knowledge. She wrote until her hand went numb and she had to massage it back to life.

After two hours, she finished the exam. Owen, who had been reading articles about Bigfoot sightings on his computer, grabbed up the pages and skimmed over her answers, nodding in approval. He scanned her test answers and emailed it to HWC headquarters, then handed her a new ID badge.

"Welcome to the Halcyon Weapons Corporation," he said, shaking her hand.

"Thanks... I think."

She clipped the badge to her lab coat.

They exited the office and headed down a hallway full of electronically sealed cabinets containing LED displays.

Owen instructed her that it was imperative that she keep her personal belongings outside the facility. She complied and locked her purse and cell phone inside one of the cabinets by using her new key card badge as the access key. Then she followed Owen to an elevator at the end of the hallway.

Mary slid her card through the reader. The elevator doors opened. They entered and went down to the basement level.

Before them stood a vast underground facility. The main corridor sprawled out before them as big as a football stadium, with different rooms specializing in all kinds of weaponry. Dozens of people rushed back and forth, some with clipboards and lab coats, others in military uniforms.

She followed Owen through the bustling crowds and continued toward one of the main units.

The sign on the door read: *Pyrotechnics.*

Inside, two men in lab coats fidgeted with a flamethrower. Plastic dummies were set up everywhere, the walls behind the dummies scorched black. Far above, ceiling fans chopped the air and swallowed the lingering smoke through ventilation shafts. Sandbags circled the two men.

Mary and Owen entered the room and navigated through the throng of sandbags. They made their way toward the center of the room. When the two men locked eyes with Mary, they rushed over, surrounding her and introducing themselves.

"I'm Colin!" the younger man said. He was tall and thin and had a crooked smile.

"I'm Robert!" the other man said, edging past his coworker. He had a small gut and large glasses and a receding hairline.

Owen regarded the two men with a look of admiration. "Both Colin and Robert are two of our top engineers. They helped create one of our bestselling smart guns. Now they've been tasked by the U.S. military to help develop a flamethrower designed as an attachment for the M-16 assault rifle. So, guys—how's it coming?"

"Horrible!" Colin said. "The fuel canisters are just too damn big. We could use charged plasma instead, but then it would be a plasma-thrower, not a flamethrower."

"Interesting," Owen said. "And just remember... I don't want to be anywhere near you when you try them out for the first time."

"Me neither," Colin said, throwing Mary a quick smile.

"What's a smart gun?" Mary asked.

Robert, who had remained mostly silent, spoke up. "It's our new line of safety firearms. Would you like to see our display?"

"I would. Thanks, Robert."

Robert beamed at her and then led them across the laboratory, past benches overflowing with nozzles and fuel tanks and other miscellaneous parts. Dozens of people scurried around the department, charting diagrams on computer screens and field testing different prototype weapons.

They entered a hallway on the opposite end of the entrance leading to a weapons display room. Dozens of handguns were displayed on the wall beneath thick glass. The firearms looked sleek and futuristic.

"First off," Owen said, "we have what's called the Sting Safety Kit. It uses a magnetized fail-safe ring, which kind of looks like a normal ring you'd wear on your finger. But when the ring comes in close proximity to the gun, it unlatches the internal safety so the gun can be fired."

"So, if a cop is ever disarmed," Mary said, "his weapon can't be used against him?"

"That's exactly right," Owen answered. He was about to pull out one of the firearms from the display, when a male voice blared loudly out of the intercom:

"Owen Ashford, line 6. It's urgent."

Owen sighed loudly. He found the nearest intercom and turned the dial to the right channel. "Hello? This is Owen."

"Owen!" the voice said through the speaker.

"Nick, is that you again? You find Phil, or what?"

"Yes, I did. But he doesn't look so hot."

"What's wrong?"

"He's dead."

"Seriously?"

"Yes, but I'm working with Dr. Cornish right now on resuscitating him."

"Well, for what it's worth, I'm sorry to hear about your friend. Did you find out anything more about this wormhole business?"

"I did, but that's confidential."

"But you've been talking about it all morning, and on an open channel."

"Oh yeah, that's right." He cleared his throat. "I'll back up a bit and explain a few things again, so everyone new to the story can get caught up."

Nick began his story.

"As you know, the wormhole was formed from part of a hyper-drive system pulled from an alien spacecraft. The drive, from our understanding, contains the ability to blur space and time, so you can slip from one point to another—kind of like opening a doorway. We think that whatever grabbed Phil was living out there in the vastness of space. And we think it became attracted to this particular doorway, like a moth to a flame."

"If that wreckage is indeed from an alien spacecraft," Owen said, "then why didn't that particular creature come through when the aliens were using it?"

"Because their doorways were used in shorter intervals. Seconds, actually."

"I see. How long have you had your doorway open?"

"Twelve years."

"What! But you just told me about it this morning! Has it been growing the entire time?"

"Yeah, but only a little bit. Especially this morning, when we cranked up the Tesla coils. We wanted to see what would happen if we put a lot of power through it."

"You have to close it!"

"No way! We can't just abandon a project in the

middle of a breakthrough! Who do you think we are, the weapons lab?" He laughed. "If whatever lurking out there sticks its head into our business, it's going to get its ass fried. I have men stationed there with plasma rifles as we speak. And don't worry, we'll work on reversing the magnetic field by the end of the year. By then we should know everything we wanted to know."

"I think you should shut down that contraption as soon as possible," Owen said. "I'll send in a security team to deal with the threat."

"I have it handled, Owen."

"But you're not a fighter, you're a scientist!"

"Tell me, who vanquished that possessed oven mitt last year? You know, the one that kept floating around and slapping the shit out of people in the kitchen? That's right, it was me! And who ate that jar of expired tomato soup and didn't get sick? That's right, it was me!"

"This is much bigger than some ghost baker or a jar of expired soup. We're talking about going head-to-head with something that lives in the darkness between space and time! Do you think you can really hurt it with just a few plasma rifles?"

"We shall see..."

The line went dead.

"It sounds like he's gone completely mad," Mary said.

"It's okay," Colin answered. "That happens at least once a week around here. Mad scientists tend to go... well... *mad* on occasion."

Chapter 3

"I think you should head to security," Owen told Colin. "I don't trust Nickolas to find his way out of a wet paper bag. Bring a squad down here. You might need to breach the laboratory." Owen turned to Robert. "I want you to fill in everyone about what's going on and then help security breach the main doors if there's resistance."

Robert nodded in agreement, then sprinted away.

Colin took two steps toward the elevator, but stopped and leveled Mary with a comforting look. "Don't worry," he said. "Shit like this happens all the time. Just last year, Dr. Cornish dropped LSD and thought he was Dr. Frankenstein. He ended up resuscitating a bunch of dead bodies from the morgue and tried to teach them how to dance to the *Footloose* soundtrack."

"Shouldn't he have picked *Thriller* instead?"

"That's what I said! But anyway, they didn't want to dance. They stormed through East Wing and ransacked the kitchen and ended up eating all the biscuits and gravy.

Don't know why, but reanimated corpses love biscuits and gravy. Then, there was this one time—"

"Time to move out," Owen said, urging him away.

"Oh yeah, right. Later!" He hoofed it toward the elevator.

Owen shook his head at Colin's antics, then motioned for Mary to follow him further down the corridor. He led her to a door named: *Gun Range and Maintenance.*

Inside, targets were set up at different intervals across a shooting range. Some of the targets were dummies wearing lab coats. An older blonde woman with her hair in a ponytail and muscular arms glanced up from dismantling a handgun and nodded to both of them, then proceeded to ignore them completely.

"Have you ever heard of a company called Nexia Biotechnologies?" Owen asked.

"No, I haven't. Who are they?"

"They are a Quebec based company. Working alongside some of our top scientists in the Genetics Department, they have successfully spliced the DNA of spiders with goats."

"For real?"

"Yes, for real."

"Why the hell would they do that?"

"Spider silk is very precious. It's used to make Kevlar for bullet-proof vests. It also contains similarities to human biology, and can be used to repair ligaments and tendons. Of course, harvesting spider silk is extremely difficult and time consuming."

Owen motioned to the shooting range. "Our scientists first tried to house the spiders in one central unit, similar in size to this gun range. But since spiders are territorial, they ended up killing each other. So, we decided on another option—of splicing their DNA with goats."

"Is it because goats *aren't* territorial?" Mary asked. "Is it because they live in herds?"

"Not really," he said, "but that's a very smart assumption. The biggest reason is because goats produce many gallons of milk every week. The changes in the DNA allowed the goats to produce spider silk instead of regular milk." [ii]

"Seriously?"

"Yes. And the studies have been very successful. We now have goats that look perfectly normal and act perfectly normal, but lactate spider silk instead of regular milk. Your lab coat, for instance, is made up of this material. It can withstand a .45 caliber slug." Owen turned to the blonde woman. "Betty, could you please demonstrate?"

The woman nodded, then expertly slapped together the handgun. She fired twice at the first dummy in a lab coat. Both shots failed to penetrate. Lead bullets clattered to the tile floor.

Mary looked down and felt the fabric of her coat with her fingertips. "Are you saying my lab coat is bullet proof?"

"Yes, and fireproof."

"Are you expecting gunfire in the facility anytime soon, Owen?"

"Let's just say it's been a strange month."

Mary was about to ask another question when a male voice called out over the loudspeaker: "Owen Ashford, line 6. It's urgent. Again."

Owen sighed. Loudly. He found an intercom system close by, took a deep breath to steady his nerves, and answered. "What now, Nick?"

"It came through the wormhole!" Nick yelled through the receiver. "Whatever that thing is—it came through and killed everyone! Then it came for me, but I got away. I always get away!"

"Nick, you're rambling like an idiot. Where are you?"

"I'm in the morgue, with Doctor Cornish."

"Have you seen the creature? What is it?"

"It's a horror from beyond the stars! Even now I can feel its power burrowing deep into my skull, trying to glean the secrets of the universe! But I won't let it!"

"Nick, have you contacted security yet? They can get a squad there to help you deal with any cosmic intruders. Colin is on his way over there. They should be able to—"

"It's too late! I sealed the doors and changed the codes! Pray it never finds a way out!"

Owen dropped the receiver and rushed outside to the massive main door leading to the Genetics Facility. He swiped his ID card through the access lock. It didn't work. He tried twice more, but to no avail.

"Open the door, Nick!" he yelled into the door intercom.

"No way! It's for your own good." His voice settled

down a bit. "I'm sorry I yelled at you earlier today, Owen. That was out of line. You wanna know something? I shouldn't have married my wife, Anne. Not at all. She used to be pretty, but now she looks a lot like that thing that slithered through the wormhole and started eating everyone. I should have married Anne's sister, Margaret, instead. She had a prettier smile, and a nicer ass." Nick's voice faded off to barely a whisper. "My wife... the horror, the horror..."

The line went dead.

Chapter 4

"Is there any other way into the research lab?" Mary asked after Nick's strange transmission.

"Nope," Owen said. "Not unless we blast a hole through the wall."

"What about that vent right above your head?"

"A vent? Preposterous! That's never worked for anyone."

Mary pried off the cover, then lifted herself inside, head first. Dust kicked up and made her cough in fits.

"It looks like I can get through here," she said. Her voice echoed through the cramped interior and sounded hollow. "I think it leads down a floor, to the morgue." [iii]

She glanced back and could see the top of Owen's head and his white eyebrows. He stood on his tiptoes, trying to see inside the shaft. "I can't fit inside, Mary. You'll have to go alone. Find Nick and get him to give you the access codes. He's a sucker for a pretty woman."

"Okay, I will."

"Also, if you're heading to the morgue, stay away from Dr. Cornish. He's completely insane."

"Roger that. I can hide pretty well, so no worries."

"Good. Be safe, and see you soon."

She slid through the shaft, then pushed out the vent cover and jumped down into the morgue. It smelled like death and chemicals.

An older man stood in front of a cadaver. He held an electric bone saw and wore a surgical mask. "Hello," he said. "I'm Doctor Cornish."

"Shit. I'll be on my way. Sorry."

"Not so fast." He set down his saw and pulled off his surgical mask. He was a handsome older man, with a thick beard containing streaks of gray that reminded her of bolts of lightning. "So, who might you be, young lady?"

"My name is Mary. I'm a new hire in the Weapons Department."

"Interesting. And why are you scurrying around in my ventilation shaft?"

"I'm looking for a physicist named Nick. The last I heard, he was in this morgue."

"Very interesting." He moved closer and pulled out a stethoscope from his pocket, then held it up to her heart. "You have a strong heartbeat. Are you an organ donor, by chance?"

"No," she lied.

"Pity," he said, draping the stethoscope around his shoulder and setting down a hammer hidden behind his back. "Are you fertile, by chance? I need to replenish my egg supply."

Mary felt herself getting a little creeped out. She thought about running to the adjacent door and booking it down the hall. But then the cadaver behind the doctor lifted up its head and stared at Dr. Cornish with pleading eyes. Actually, it looked kinda pissed. It tried to stand, but its stomach spilled out all over the place, the entrails unraveling and feeding itself like an uncoiling rope.

Dr. Cornish gasped. He ran to the cadaver in blind panic. With hammer in hand, he thumped the corpse on the head a few times until it settled back down. Then he regarded Mary with a maniacal grin and lifted his hands in front of him, as if ready to choke her. "Now it's time to deal with you, my little trespasser. You need to pay!"

"Pay for what?" she said, challengingly.

"For trespassing in my morgue! This is top secret stuff, you know!"

"Okay. How's fifty bucks sound?"

"What? Seriously?"

"Yup. I'll send it over right now. You have a PayPal account, right?"

"I do."

"What's your email address?"

"It's <u>corpsesbcrazy@gmail.com</u>." [iv]

Mary went to the desk computer, opened a browser, typed in her password, and opened her account. She entered the total and sent over the cash. "Done!" she said.

The doctor sat down at his terminal and logged into

his account. "Wonderful! The transaction says it's in progress. So, what now?"

"Now, you show me your work."

"Of course! Let's see, how about we start in the Cryogenics Lab? Or how about the Tower of Resuscitation?"

"First, I want to know where that horrible smell is coming from."

Dr. Cornish's smile slipped, fell. "What smell?"

Mary didn't answer. She walked through the morgue to the other side of the room. The smell wasn't coming from the cadaver on the operating table. The smell emanated from the Cryogenics Lab. The door stood wide open.

Inside the lab, dozens of bodies were in pristine-looking cryogenic chambers. Computer terminals monitored bio-rhythms and cellular activity. Despite the cleanliness of the lab, the horrid smell still lingered.

On the far side of the laboratory, behind a thick plate-glass window, two men in white uniforms monitored the frozen bodies. They held clipboards and chatted with each other, silently.

"I don't smell anything," Dr. Cornish said, walking up behind her. "The bodies are frozen at -380 degrees. There's no cellular damage at all, so it can't be—"

"It's not the frozen bodies. It's something rotting. You don't smell that?"

"No." He inhaled deeply. "It smells like fresh spring trees."

"What's in here?" Mary said, opening a closet door.

Flies and rats swarmed out in a hellish plague, revealing a mountain of decomposing body parts. Some were freshly dead, while others were skeletons picked clean by maggots and insects. Rows of dirty jars held eyeballs and brains and testicles.

"What the fucking hell is all this?" she asked.

"It's nothing!"

"No... it's something. You have to get rid of these!"

"No way," Dr. Cornish said. "You see Stanley here? He was my first operation when I was twenty years old. And Regina, the one closest to you... she was my first leg transplant. And Richard was my first lobotomy."

"You know what you are, Dr. Cornish?"

"What?"

"You're a body part hoarder."

"Am not."

"Well, I don't have time for your bullshit. We're being attacked by an alien lifeform hell-bent on world domination. It's heading toward the Genetics Lab and moving closer this way. You and your staff are in danger."

"Oh, that... right. I saw it on the footage downloaded from the security feed."

"Wait a minute... you *saw* it?"

"Yeah. Nick went a little bonkers when I showed it to him. Honestly, I don't see what all the fuss is about. The thing looks like a fat octopus with wings."

"Is it because you're already mad, so seeing it has no effect on you?"

"Interesting hypothesis. But I think it's because I've seen something similar before. My two lab assistants keep praying to a statue that resembles it."

Mary glanced at the two lab assistants. Both men smiled and waved. She imitated the sentiment and waved back. "Dr. Cornish," she whispered, "do you think it's possible your lab assistants are in a cult?"

"Hmmm. That's another interesting hypothesis. And it would also explain that shipment of false idols I received last week."

"Do you know where Nick is now, Dr. Cornish?"

"He's in the Genetics Lab trying to track down the creature. I can show you how to get there, if you like."

"Great. And just so you know, this little hoarding problem isn't over yet. Trust me, it's not good to surround yourself with your failures. Dwelling on your past prevents you from moving toward your future."

Dr. Cornish was about to say something, but stopped himself. "You know what? That makes a lot of sense. You're very pragmatic, Mary. Out of curiosity, could you possibly help me with something in my lab?"

"Help you with what?"

"I need help interrogating a prisoner. The information might prove valuable to your mission."

"Lead the way."

Chapter 5

Mary followed Dr. Cornish from the Cryogenics Laboratory back into the morgue. He ushered her over to the cadaver. Mary sidestepped the blood and guts and stood next to the doctor. She waited patiently.

"Do you know how this man died?" Dr. Cornish asked.

"Is it because you hit him in the head with a hammer?"

"No, I mean the first time."

"I don't. Was he donated to your lab?"

"No. Just this morning he was pulled through an interdimensional wormhole."

"I see. So, this is Phillip?"

"It is, yes. He helped bring that monstrosity into our facility. He also locked me inside my own lab, then let one of my genetically altered animals loose, hoping it would kill me. That's why I acted so hostile toward you earlier. My apologies, Mary."

"No harm done."

"That's good to hear. Thank you."

"What kind of animal did he let loose?"

"It was a badger. And not just any badger. I did a series of transplants to give it opposable thumbs. It's a breakthrough of modern science."

"But, if you gave it opposable thumbs, couldn't it have gotten out by itself, considering it could now open doors? Maybe even lock you in your own morgue?"

The doctor gave her a wide-eyed look. "I didn't think of that."

Mary continued. "Speaking of doorways, how did the alien get inside the research lab in the first place? Weren't there armed men guarding the wormhole?"

"There were, but from what I understand, they went missing. I don't know for certain, but I think Phillip had something to do with their disappearance." He leaned down closer to the cadaver and pointed. "See this mark?"

Mary noticed a patch of skin on the cadaver's ribs, and a tattoo that read:

Yig-Sothoth for ~~life~~ eternity.

"What does that mean?" she asked.

"I asked Marcy about it. She works in the Archives Department on the top floor. She did some research and found out that Yig-Sothoth is a Starspawn of Cthulhu. She also uncovered valuable information about how to conquer this creature. Get this, the secret weapon is... *peanut butter!*"

"What? Are you fucking mad?"

"A little, yes."

"So, let me get this straight—an ancient and all-powerful cosmic creature named Yig-Sothoth, has traveled countless eons across space and time, and its one weakness is peanut butter?"

"Yes. Exactly!"

"What clue did your friend find?"

"She uncovered a scroll with the letters *Pb* inscribed on it. It is rumored to be the only element that can hurt creatures *born of the stars*."

"Doesn't *Pb* stand for *lead* on the *Periodic Table of Elements*?"

"Really? Is it the same kind of metal used in bullets?"

"Yes."

"Interesting. This creature is getting harder and harder to kill by the second. As of now, I've been tasked with trying to figure out more by reanimating Phillip and questioning him. Now that you're here, I'll require your assistance."

"Okay. Where do we start?"

"First, we have to make sure another spirit hasn't entered his body. There's plenty of ghosts on the loose in this part of the facility. Just so you know—when you walk around, watch your step. Things become possessed very quickly. That includes people, so breathe through your nose."

"Okay, I'll remember. And let's get this done quickly."

"Agreed." Dr. Cornish bent over and injected Phillip with a purple-colored serum. Then the doctor crossed his arms and waited. Nothing happened. He shook the dead man by the shoulders and waited. Still nothing. Finally, he hooked up a car battery and zapped him in the head.

Phillip's eyes snapped opened. "I smell oranges."

"That's because you have a tumor," Dr. Cornish said. "I keep telling you that. But I suppose it doesn't matter now, considering you're dead. You got pulled through a wormhole and died."

"I remember. I also remember waking up and seeing you talking to a young, pretty woman." His eyes fixed on Mary. "Hey... there she is. Hello."

"Hello," Mary said, politely.

"After that," Phillip continued, "I tried to stand up, but something knocked me out cold."

"A hammer fell on you," the doctor said.

"I hate when that happens. Why can't I move?"

"You're strapped down for your protection. Now, I want you to answer my questions honestly, otherwise you'll encounter more falling hammers." Dr. Cornish cracked his knuckles and gave a maniacal grin. "Tell me... who am I communicating with?"

"Phillip."

"Phillip who?"

"I'm not telling you my last name."

"Why not?"

"Because."

"Is it because a malicious spirit has entered your body, and you don't know the answer?"

"No. It's because you never remember my last name.

And when someone reminds you, you make fun of me."

"I would never do that."

"His name is Phillip Sherry," Mary said, pointing to the dead man's shirt. "His ID badge is clipped to his jacket."

"Sherry!" Dr. Cornish said, flicking the name badge. "That's it! So, tell me... why is your last name a woman's first name instead of a real last name?"

Phillip started looking angry. "Don't make fun of my last name. You always do that!"

"Then answer my question."

"No!"

"Why not?"

"Because I don't want to!"

The doctor grinned. "Technically by saying 'I don't want to,' you're answering my question."

The dead man started jiggling his wrist restraints. "Stop it! I can't take any more of your stupid logic traps! Let me outta here!"

"I can't do that. My serum has brought you back to life, so you must heed my words. You must do as I command!"

"I won't! Dr. West's animation serum doesn't work like that. Everyone knows that!"

Dr. Cornish looked panicked. "What do I do, Mary?" The doctor's hand involuntarily crept toward the hammer on the tray.

Mary thought for a moment. "You know what sounds good, doctor?"

"What?"

"Biscuits and gravy."

Phillip's face snapped toward her like a dog locked onto the scent of a cheeseburger, but then he gave a sour look. "That won't work on me. I don't have a stomach anymore. See?" He pointed to his intestines.

Mary ignored him. "Dr. Cornish, would you please fetch us some biscuits and gravy from the kitchen?"

"Gladly." The doctor ran out of the room. Then he returned a few minutes later holding two heaping plates full of food. He handed one plate to her, then began spooning the food into his mouth.

Mary was hungry and the biscuits tasted great. But she forced herself to only eat half. The whole time she ate, Phillip stared at her with pleading eyes. He licked his lips and drooled.

"You know what?" Mary said. "I guess I'm not hungry after all." She began dumping the remaining food into the garbage bin, slowly and dramatically.

"No!" Phillip cried. "You're wasting it!"

"Then tell us what we want to know," she said. "Who is Yig-Sothoth?"

"She's an ancient goddess! She's traveled light years to come and find me! And soon we'll be together for eternity!"

"Ew," Dr. Cornish said, wiping his mouth on his sleeve. He set his empty plate down. "You know what she looks like, don't you?"

"Of course, I do. She revealed herself to me in my

dreams. She's Swedish looking, with long blonde hair, pale skin, large breasts, and full pouty lips."

"That's Scarlet Johansson."

"No! You're just jealous!"

The doctor hit a video feed on his desk computer and angled the screen toward Phillip. "This is a video surveillance recording from this morning. Mary, avert your eyes. I don't want you going bonkers."

Mary agreed. She didn't want to go bonkers, like Nick, so she turned away and stared at the floor, although she wanted very badly to see what this creature looked like.

Strange sounds emanated from the speakers, similar to a child slurping up spaghetti and laughing hysterically at the same time.

"No!" Phillip cried. "No, it can't be! She's ugly, and gross!"

Dr. Cornish turned off the recording, then informed Mary that the possible threat to her sanity had passed.

"She lied to me," Philip said, sadly. "Why would she do that?"

"All women lie," Dr. Cornish said. "They lie with their makeup, they lie with their push-up bras, and they lie with their stupid faces. Your girlfriend is nothing more than a flat-chested octopus with wings. That's all."

"But I had a dinner reservation at Red Lobster. She was going to meet my parents." Phillip went into deep thought for a moment. "Actually, she did get kinda mad when I said I was going to order the calamari. Do you think they're related or something?"

The doctor arched his eyebrow, then said in a quizzical manner, "Yes?"

Phillip looked furious. "You know what? Screw her! You guys wanna get a pizza and some beers or something? I'm buying. Oh wait... shit, I can't eat or drink anything. Tell you what, if you put my stomach backtogether, [sick] I'll tell you everything you wanna know." [v]

"Deal," Dr. Cornish said, grinning.

"And you have to laser remove my tattoo as well."

"Yes, but you better spill the beans about everything."

"Okay, I'll spill the beans."

The dead man cleared his throat and began his story...

Chapter 6

"The alien craft was first brought to our research facility twelve years ago, around the time I was first hired as an experimental physicist by the Halcyon Weapons Corporation. The engine was one small part of a much larger wreckage, containing an alien body, a spacecraft, and a trunk full of glass jars—the meaning of which I'll explain shortly. It was found by a team of Russian oil drillers working in the Himalayas and buried deep within the ice. They excavated the items and put them on eBay and sold them to our corporation for a case of vodka and an all-expense paid trip to Vegas.

"Upon testing the alien DNA, we found the tissue samples to be a direct match with samples already in our database. This particular alien, called a Mi-Go, is a crustacean-looking creature with leathery wings and a body resembling a bloated shrimp. They are vastly intelligent creatures known to specialize in interdimensional travel. They also worship a powerful

Outer God, so we make it a point to stay on their good side and not interfere with their exploration of our solar system.

"From what we gleaned from the alien wreckage, this particular Mi-Go stopped by Earth to pick up a bunch of humans for a little joy ride around Pluto, but it must have had problems with its navigational system and crashed. Human physiology can't handle interdimensional travel, and so the Mi-Go devised a system of travel for humans which involves beheading and keeping the brain alive in a stasis container—hence, the glass jars. They love to bring like-minded specimens to their home world to learn about science and physics and to record different languages. They even keep the brains as pets after.

"As you might imagine, the head-in-a-jar transportation system didn't cause excitement amongst our peers. So, we began experimenting with the miscellaneous engine parts to see if we could replicate their sophisticated technology. Using Tesla coils on the ion-charged engine, we managed to open a small wormhole roughly the size of a half-dollar in diameter. We called this portal Experiment Portal X.

"I studied this wormhole for five years, trying to figure out how it bent space and time. By my calculations, I came to the conclusion that it uses a highly sophisticated form of time dilation, but I'm not entirely certain even to this day. Also, right around this time, I began hearing a voice in my head. I brushed it off as nonsense at first, thinking it was due to lack of sleep. But it continued, and eventually grew more persistent.

"As the months wore on, and as the voice became more and more frequent, my demeanor changed drastically. I began to think one of those pesky ghosts in the kitchen was the culprit. But when I went home at night and drifted off to sleep, I started seeing non-Euclidian ruins rising out of alien swampland and strange-looking glyphs embedded in alien structures. It was quite disturbing, and I knew it wasn't from a simple haunting or demonic possession.

"Eventually, others in the lab started having similar dreams, and we soon found solace in each other. We became good friends outside of work. We discussed many possibilities about what it could be. And then as the months passed and as our visions become more and more severe, we realized the dreams and visions were emanating from within the wormhole. By keeping it open for so long, it had become a transponder of sorts, sending out a signal across space and time. And something was answering our call.

"I started getting headaches more often. Then I started drinking heavily to make them stop. But nothing worked unless I gave in and communicated with this cosmic entity. So, I did... I let it in. It entered my dreams and came to me in the form of Scarlett Johansson and told me I should recruit others to help her return to Earth. She yearned to awaken the Old God Cthulhu—an ancient creature slumbering deep in the Pacific Ocean. She told me if I helped her, she would reward me beyond my wildest dreams.

"So, I agreed, mainly because she was really hot. The morning after I agreed to her deal, I bought new clothes and signed up for a gym membership. I also formed an online fan appreciation group dedicated to helping her return to Earth. As of now, we have dozens of followers in our group, and we've raised hundreds of dollars to help her with rent when she arrives. We have waited patiently for her return, and now, she has come!"

Chapter 7

Phillip ended his story. "Now can I have some biscuits and gravy?"

"Not so fast," Mary said. "Weren't you pulled through a wormhole earlier today? Tell us about that. Why did she suddenly attack you?"

"Well, a guy can only wait so long, am I right? She kept giving me the runaround, so I got a little pissed and started chucking rocks and beakers at her. It must have made her mad, because the next thing I knew I was being dragged from my office through that stupid hole. You know what? Outer space is really cold. After that I don't remember anything."

"Interesting," Mary said. "So, I guess the bottom line is this—you're in a doomsday cult trying to bring back an Old God."

"It's not a doomsday cult. It's more of a fan appreciation group."

"But don't you worship a Starspawn of Cthulhu?"

"Yeah, but it's not really a cult. Once in a while we get together and sing songs from *The Hymnbook of Mad Abdul Alhazred*. And sometimes we have arts and crafts day and make false idols and then go out for dinner after. That's about it."

"What's your fan appreciation group called?"

"The Followers of Yig-Sothoth."

"And are there more of your followers working in this facility?"

"Yes, at least twenty. Maybe more."

"How do we locate them?"

"I'd look for anyone wearing black ceremonial robes underneath their coats. Also, look for animal sacrifices or anyone worshiping weird-looking stone idols."

Mary glanced at Dr. Cornish. From the expression on his face, he seemed disturbed from this new information. But he also seemed content with her cross-examination. Now they had the information they needed.

Dr. Cornish walked to the intercom system and called the head of security. "Hello, Rebecca?"

"Doctor Cornish, is that you?"

"Yes, it's me."

"Nice to hear from you! I'm single again, just so you know."

"That's wonderful. Say, I think we have a code green on our hands."

"Oh-my-fucking-god!" she said, then yelled to her coworkers, "Hey everyone... dinosaurs are attacking the facility!"

"No, no... wait!" Dr. Cornish said. "That's not it. What's the code for a cult invasion?"

"That depends. What cult are you talking about?"

"The Followers of Yig-Sothoth."

"Don't know about that one. And what's a Yig-Sothoth?"

"It's a Starspawn of Cthulhu."

"Well, Cthulhu is kinda popular with the kids nowadays, so that would be just a simple code yellow. As far as organizations go, let's see... maybe they're affiliated with That Which Has Finally Been Named, or You Have a Friend in R'yleh."

Dr. Cornish turned to Phillip. "What cult are you affiliated with?"

"It's not a cult. I keep trying to tell you guys that! It's a—"

Suddenly his eyes went wide.

"What's wrong?" Mary asked.

"It's Yig-Sothoth," he said. "She has awakened from her afternoon nap! And she's pissed at me for spilling the beans!"

Blood began trickling from Phillip's nose. Then he started to convulse, his wrist restraints digging into the flesh of his arms. He stopped moving.

Dr. Cornish worked quickly. He tried to reanimate him with the defibrillator and serum until thick plumes of smoke spiraled toward the rafters and gave off the pungent smell of burnt hair. But it was no use. Phillip was gone.

Dr. Cornish said a quick prayer. He pulled a sheet over Phillip's body.

"How can this creature kill people who are already dead?" he asked after some time had passed. "Is she some sort of cosmic anti-necromancer?"

Mary shook her head. "I don't know. But we're in some deep shit. We're locked inside a part of the facility controlled by a Starspawn of Cthulhu. At any moment, she could come bursting in here and kill us. Or maybe send her cronies in to kill us instead."

Just then, the two lab assistants from the Cryogenics Lab entered the morgue. They slid on Phillip's guts and tumbled to the ground and pulled themselves up and started walking around the morgue, trying to look as nonchalant as possible.

"We need to find Nick," Mary whispered to the doctor, keeping the two newcomers far away. "We need to get the access codes for the main door."

"Right," Dr. Cornish said. "Let's slip out while we can."

Just then, a transmission went live on the intercom:

"Attention everyone. This is Rebecca, head of security here at HWC. I'm issuing a code yellow. Recently, we've been alerted to cult activity within the facility. This group of degenerate assholes, who call themselves The Followers of Yig-Sothoth, are complete fucking shit-heads. If you witness anyone wearing robes or conducting animal sacrifices, please contact us immediately. This cult is trying to wake up old Squid-

Head himself, so don't wait until the end of the month to file a report. Do it immediately. And a special thanks to Dr. Cornish for figuring this one out. Love you, Doctor! Over and out."

"Wow, that girl's totally into you," Mary said.

"Rebecca?" he asked.

"Yup."

"Really?"

"She'd give you as many eggs as you wanted for your weird experiments."

The two lab techs now stood before them, their coats crumpled on the floor. They wore black robes, previously hidden under their lab coats. They also held curved daggers.

"I agree," the first cultist said. "Rebecca's totally into you, doctor."

"Absolutely," the second cultist said. "And she has that whole sexy librarian thing going on, too." He smiled. "By the way, Yig-Sothoth sends her regards."

Suddenly, from the corner of the morgue, a vent cover clattered to the ground. It caused them all to jump. And then something dropped to the floor and waddled out into the light.

The (escaped?) badger.

To Mary, the animal looked pissed and hungry. It had a necklace of rat ears around its neck. It seemed it had been out hunting in the air vents, and hunting well.

"Toby!" the doctor cried. "Please help us!"

Toby couldn't answer the doctor, because he was just

a badger, but he must have understood the direness of the situation at some level, because he flicked open a switchblade and snarled at the intruders.

The cultists tried to flee, but it was too late.

Chapter 8

Dr. Cornish led Mary out of the morgue and through a labyrinth of interconnected hallways and corridors. From behind, she could hear the cultists screaming like banshees feuding over a twilight graveyard. Then everything went silent.

They moved toward the elevator. Dr. Cornish pressed the call button. Nothing.

High above, in the rafters, the lights flickered and went out. The emergency lights kicked on and illuminated everything in a dull amber pallor. It wasn't much light, but it proved better than navigating through the darkness. Hopefully the power outage didn't happen throughout the whole facility.

"We're sitting ducks out here," Mary said. "We need weapons."

"I couldn't agree more," the doctor replied. "Follow me... to the cafeteria!"

"Why the cafeteria?"

"For PB&J sandwiches, of course!"

"What about real weapons?"

"Don't you remember our little conversation about the creature's weakness being peanut butter?"

"It's not peanut butter!"

"Yes, it is! Trust me!" He sprinted down the hallway.

Mary sighed, then followed him.

The cafeteria smelled like carrots and broccoli and fried chicken. Tables and chairs were upended. Food trays scattered across the tile. Spaghetti sauce splattered across the walls. Not a soul around, which seemed strange, considering it was around lunchtime. Maybe the employees had already fled to safety.

She followed the doctor through a set of swinging doors and into the kitchen. There, he began placing slices of bread on the counter, following it up with heaps of peanut butter and jelly. He whistled the whole time. When he finished, he stacked five sandwiches on top of each other and placed them in baggies.

"There," he said. "All done. She won't know what hit her."

"Why add the strawberry jelly?"

"Oh. Well, I figure if we get hungry, we'll also have a snack to eat, right?"

"Makes sense. But remember, it won't hurt humans like Phillip."

"Damn, you're right." He went into thought. "There's a small arms room one level up, over on the Genetics floor. It's usually stocked with rifles and ammo for just this type of emergency. What do you say?"

"Now you're talking."

The doctor grabbed his bagged sandwiches. They moved toward the Genetics Department, skirting up a flight of stairs and making their way down the twisting corridors. Mary turned a corner and walked straight into a nightmare.

Mutilated bodied littered the hallways. Dozens of bodies ripped to shreds.

"Looks like the Genetics Department staff," the doctor said, inspecting a few ID badges. "Probably trying to get to safe ground when..." He didn't finish the sentence. He didn't know how to finish the sentence.

Dr. Cornish stepped through the maze of body parts, weaving through torsos and legs. Mary followed. She could smell blood and excrement and tried not to vomit.

The doctor halted at an electronically sealed door. He fumbled with his ID and slid it through the reader. The electronic door clicked from LOCKED to OPEN.

They entered.

Instead of rifles and ammunition, human arms were strewn across the floor, freshly ripped from the bodies outside. On the wall, written in blood, was the phrase:

Arms room ☺

"I should have seen that coming," Mary said.

Dr. Cornish grimaced. "Do you think Rebecca's broadcast triggered all this?"

"It's possible. But I think the attack would have happened regardless of the transmission. There's an intercom on the wall. Let's check in."

"Right." Dr. Cornish punched the intercom button and sent out a transmission over a few open channels. He tried for many minutes, but raised only static through the receiver.

Finally, a voice answered. "Hello?"

"Hello," the doctor said. "Who's this?"

"It's Owen. Who is this?"

"Owen... this is Dr. Cornish!"

"Hello, doctor! You haven't seen a woman named Mary, by chance, have you?"

"Yes. She's here with me now."

Mary called out. "Hello, Owen!"

"Mary? Thank god, you're alive! The followers attacked right after the broadcast."

"I know. Are Robert and Colin okay?"

"They're alive and well. The intruders were met with extreme resistance—mainly a whole lab of overworked staff armed with flamethrowers."

"Good to hear! Are you safe now?"

"Yup, we're in the lobby, near the main doors. Most of the workers got out in time, but a few of us remained. None of the elevators seem to be working anymore. The Genetics floor was hit pretty hard, from what I hear."

"We're there now. It's not pretty."

"I see. You have any luck reaching Nick yet?"

"No. We're trying to find him. Dr. Cornish is helping me."

"Wait a minute... Dr. Cornish is *helping* you?"

"Yes. He's become quite a good friend."

"But... isn't he insane?"

"A little, yes."

Dr. Cornish leaned over to Mary, then whispered, quite loudly, "Tell him I'm getting better."

"He's getting better," she said.

"Well, I'm glad to hear it. I think we should—"

The line cut out.

"Owen, are you there? Hello?" She tried flipping the receiver to other channels, cranking the knob in different directions, but nothing else came through.

Suddenly, footsteps reverberated through the facility. They were loud as hell and shook the walls, as if a small explosion had detonated nearby. Dust kicked up from the ceiling and floated through the air in a chalky mist.

And then something LARGE slithered into view.

Instantly, Mary knew she was looking at Yig-Sothoth, the ancient Starspawn of Cthulhu. And it didn't look a thing like Scarlett Johansson, either. It gave off some sort of electromagnetic pulse, affecting the emergency lights and causing them to flicker in machinegun bursts. But through the darkness, she could still make out a few characteristics, mainly a gigantic scaled body and eyes that looked like falling stars. Tentacles swarmed from its mouth and reminded her of starving sea lamprey. Its massive body stood on tree trunk legs and its hands were webbed and held claws that could tear through cement and steel. It looked like a creature assembled out of ten other creatures.

Mary felt an uncontrollable urge to scream. Her mind began spiraling into the world of dreams. She fought to regain control of her senses, but it was too late. She felt the walls of her reality began to melt—as if every single thing she had ever known throughout her entire life didn't matter. She felt helpless in front of such an ancient creature. She felt obsolete and powerless.

The Starspawn held out its arms and bellowed in an inhuman rage. Then it charged down the hallway, each footstep reverberating through the floor and striking Mary's body like a shotgun blast to her chest. She was vaguely aware of Dr. Cornish pitching a sandwich at it, and the sandwich bouncing off the creature, harmlessly. But that was about it.

And then something strange happened.

The creature stopped charging. It held one hand to the concrete wall in support, then started wheezing in and out. At first Mary thought the sandwich had caused the strange reaction. But that wasn't possible. Then she realized something—something she had seen many times in patients while working as a respiratory therapist.

Yig-Sothoth had asthma. [vi]

And then Dr. Cornish grabbed her by her shoulders and shook her until she regained her wits. "Run!" he yelled.

She ran.

Chapter 9

Mary ran until her lungs felt like exploding. Her vision blurred and she knew she was on the verge of fainting. She fought it off for as long as she could, but a soft ringing in her ears caused her to lose her equilibrium. She felt her body falling to the ground in slow motion. And then she was dreaming.

She woke on the tile floor. Dr. Cornish sat on the floor beside her, eating a sandwich. Although the Starspawn's coughing still echoed throughout the facility, the intensity had lessened considerably.

"You okay?" the doctor asked.

"I think... yes. But my head is killing me."

"It'll pass. Fainting is a normal reaction to seeing a Starspawn. Actually, I'm surprised you remained conscious for as long as you did. When Nick saw the creature for the first time, he fainted instantly. You'll have to let me study your brainwaves sometime."

"Sure, whatever." She stood up. "Where are we?"

"You don't remember?"

"No."

"We're at the Experimental Physics laboratory. The entrance is right down the hall."

"Wait a minute... are you saying we made it?"

"Yes, we made it."

"Then help me up. We need to hurry!"

Dr. Cornish gulped down the rest of his sandwich, then helped her up and they moved cautiously toward the lab entrance. Mary pushed on the intercom. Nothing but static. She pushed again and this time the door opened and three men armed with M-16 assault rifles rushed out. Mary and Dr. Cornish were surrounded in seconds.

"What are you doing here?" a voice called out from the doorway.

Mary instantly recognized Nick's voice. He exited the lab right behind his men. He was much better looking than she would have thought, with clear blue eyes and a lean build. The handle of a Glock handgun jutted out from his belt.

"I'll ask you both again," Nick said. "What are you doing here?"

"We're here to seal the wormhole," the doctor said.

"A hopeless task," Nick answered. He walked up to Dr. Cornish and looked him right in the eyes. "If I remember correctly, the last time we met, you showed me a video of that disgusting creature eating a janitor. Tell me something, doctor... was that intentional? Did you want to drive me insane?"

"No. I just thought it would be funny to record your reaction and upload it to YouTube."

"Wait a minute... you recorded me?"

"Yes."

"How many views so far?"

"Over a thousand."

"Whoa... nice!" He turned to Mary. "And who is this?"

"This is Mary," the doctor said. "She's a new hire in the Weapons Department."

"Very nice," Nick said, devouring her cleavage and legs with his eyes. "Let me guess—you're here because Owen wants me to shut down the wormhole?"

"Correct," she said, not bothering to lie.

"Tell me... wouldn't that trap the Starspawn here with us? Wouldn't that make things worse, considering the creature is immortal, and cannot die?"

"That's a good point," she said. "Do you have a better plan? I'd love to hear it."

"Yes, I do. I..." A panicked look fell over his face.

"I'm listening," Mary said.

"Give me a sec!" He went into thought for a minute, then shook his head in defeat. "Dammit! I can't think! Something is blocking my thoughts." He looked about ready to freak out. "Maybe it's you, Mary? Are you toying with my mind?"

"How am I doing that?"

"With that sultry smile and those gorgeous legs! Any second now you're going to sprout tentacles and try to kill me! Look out, men! Get her in your sights!"

Mary needed to handle this quickly and carefully. "Who handles the HVAC work around here?"

"What the hell are you talking about?" Nick yelled. "I've never even heard of such a thing... *HVAC!* Or is that more evil gibberish? Are you casting a spell on us?"

"I'm talking about the heating, ventilation, and air conditioning. Do you have a team that regulates the temperature? Is it forced air?"

"Yeah, so?"

"So, if it were up to me, I'd open up all the doors between here and the Genetics Department and try to lead the Starspawn back to this spot. From what I've witnessed, it's having trouble acclimating to our atmosphere. I'd use the ventilation shafts to blow as much dust around as possible. Once the creature arrives, we can push it through to the other side and seal the wormhole shut by destroying the power grid."

"That's a pretty good plan," one of the armed men said.

"I agree," the second man said.

"Maybe we should follow her from now on," the third man said.

The three officers formed a huddle. They whispered something and then nodded in agreement. Then they walked over and stood behind Mary, protecting their new leader. Dr. Cornish offered them each a sandwich. From the smiles on their faces, they were won over for good.

"Dammit!" Nick said, fuming at the loss of his men. He pulled out his Glock and just kind of waved it around.

"What do you know? You haven't stared into the darkness like I have! It will consume you! It will consume you all!"

He pointed the gun at Mary, and she responded.

She struck Nick in the wrist. The gun clattered to the floor. Then she threw him to the ground with a hip throw, dropping him on the spot. Overall, it was a well-executed Judo move.

Nick tried to regain his balance. He wobbled to his feet and was about to say something, but fell back down. He just sat there and stared up at her, as if he were a confused infant waiting for a parent to pick him up and comfort him.

"I'm sorry, Mary," he said. "I don't know what came over me."

"It's not your fault," she said, helping him up. She picked up his handgun and then turned to the others. "We're fighting something powerful, something from beyond the stars. It can alter your thoughts in the blink of an eye, and it can turn friends into foes. We have to trust each other from now on. We need unity."

Murmurs went around the small group, all in agreement.

"Dr. Cornish," she said, singling him out, "I need you to get the access codes from Nick and then head to the main doors at the east facility. I want you to manually open the doors and get Owen and his team to occupy the lower floors. Have them push the creature this way with their plasma rifles and flamethrowers. After that, I want you to head up to the control room and convince Rebecca to call in their best HVAC staff. We need to seal off the departments and generate more heat and dust. We're going to funnel the creature back to the portal room."

"Are you and Nick going to set a trap for it there?" Dr. Cornish said.

"That's right. I have a plan."

"Sounds good to me." The doctor pulled out a piece of paper and a pen and handed it over to Nick.

Nick grabbed the items and wrote the main security passcode down and handed it back over. Mary stole a glance and noticed the password was simply: NICK. Then the doctor gave Mary a grin and was off, moving toward the genetics lab. He sang a little song to himself, possibly not realizing he was walking straight into danger once again.

Mary turned to the three officers. "I want you guys to follow the doctor. He's the only one capable of fending off an attack from the creature. If he fails, we're in serious trouble. Protect him with your lives."

All three men saluted her. And then they were gone.

Chapter 10

Nick rounded on Mary as soon as they were alone. The look on his face conveyed pure horror. "How are we going to push a Starspawn back into an interdimensional wormhole?"

Mary shrugged. "I'm not sure. Any suggestions?"

"How about a battering ram?"

"Hmmm."

"I know! A battering ram attached to a tank!"

"We don't have the time for that."

Nick went into thought, then pulled out a metal flask from his pocket. He took a long swig and went into deep contemplation.

Mary grabbed the flask out of his hands and swallowed a mouthful. It was just normal tap water, but it tasted refreshing. She handed it back. "Think you can show me this wormhole now?"

"Yeah, I suppose. The walk will give me time to think. But we'll have to be careful. It's very unstable, and growing bigger by the second." He grinned, then added, "Kind of like my wife."

"I'll be careful of both. Lead the way."

Nick ushered her into the Experimental Physics laboratory. They shuffled past a dozen offices and observatories containing expensive machinery.

"You can probably feel the wormhole already," Nick said. "The static vibrations? It's using a lot of power."

"I can feel it on my arms. Is that why the power went out earlier?"

"It is. I had to reroute the main power to keep the wormhole operational, otherwise it would be trapped here in this facility with us."

"Good thinking, Nick."

"Thanks."

Nick stopped at a doorway, reading: *Experiment Portal Room X*. He slid his card through the reader.

From inside, chanting.

Mary pulled out Nick's handgun and moved inside the room. It was dark and she stumbled through machine parts, swearing with each stub of her foot. It looked like somebody had taken apart a car motor and placed it in rows on the floor. Then she realized the pieces weren't from a car at all, but made of a strange-looking filament that resembled durable tin foil. Probably from the alien craft found by the team of Russians.

The moved closer. The chanting grew louder.

They climbed a towering set of stairs and entered a part of the building as big as an amphitheater. The ceiling was full of metal girders holding ceiling fans the size of windmill blades. A control room hung suspended from the ceiling, three floors up. The air held a strange energy, like a lightning storm on the horizon.

They ducked behind a shipping crate and watched.

In the center of the laboratory stood a black sphere twenty feet in diameter. Fog weaved around it like orbiting snakes. The sphere pulsed faintly, and Mary could see stars blinking on the other side. It was a beautiful sight to behold, if oddly surreal.

In front of the sphere, a group of cultists stood, dressed in black hoods, chanting and holding their false idol statues to their chests.

"They're trying to close the portal," Nick whispered. "We have to stop them."

"Okay, this is a Glock 19, so I have fifteen shots total," she said. "Looks like I can miss three times and still have enough to take them all out."

"Fifteen shots?" Nick said, surprised.

"Yes."

"In the gun?"

"Yes. Why are you so surprised?"

"Nothing."

"Did you load it?"

"Yes."

"Did you load fifteen bullets into the mag?"

"The mag?"

"The bottom piece, right here?"

"No. I just stuck a bullet in the barrel."

Mary ejected the magazine and then checked the gun's chamber. "Seriously, Nick? One bullet? Are you that clueless?"

"How am I supposed to know a gun holds more than one bullet?"

"Because we don't live in the 1700s anymore!"

"Well, maybe I do! You don't know me! We just met like twenty minutes ago!"

At this point, Mary was about to really give it to him. But then she realized a few things. First, the main reason they were acting so hostile toward each other definitely had to do with Nick's limited knowledge of firearms. But it also had to do with the sweltering heat blasting through the facility. Also, she could hear the sound of explosions and cough-bombs going off in the distance. It looked like Dr. Cornish had succeeded in his mission and was driving the creature back to its point of origin. She also realized that Nick was yelling so loudly, the cultists were now alerted to their presence.

"Don't move!" Mary said, holding up the gun to the crowd forming around them.

One cultist strode forward and lifted back his hood. He was middle-aged and with a greying beard. "Go ahead," he said. "We all heard you arguing, so we know you only have one bullet. Now, why don't you put down your gun and join us in our daily worship? Repeat after me: *Yig-Sothoth shows no mercy—*"

"Wait a minute," Mary said. "Why worship her if she shows no mercy? That seems weird."

"You didn't let me finish," he said. *"Yig-Sothoth shows no mercy... to non-believers."* He paused and breathed in deeply through his nose. "Now repeat after me."

"Hold on," she said. "Isn't that a double negative?"

"I don't know!" he said, throwing his hands up in the air and dropping his stone idol. "Bah! You're as bad as Dr. Cornish with your confusing rhetoric! And look what you made me do? You made me drop my idol!"

"Was it expensive?"

A huge grin crept across his face. "Why don't you ask Yig-Sothoth yourself?" He pointed to the door behind her.

Mary turned, slowly.

Yig-Sothoth stood behind her, tapping a clawed foot and holding a struggling Nick in one hand. The ancient creature was covered in blood and gore and Mary thought she could see a human foot stuck deep within its molars. Then the Starspawn roared and spread its wings and reached down with its other hand to squeeze the life out of Mary.

But instead... Yig-Sothoth's eyes went wide.

The furnace blasted it right in the face with hot air. It sneezed.

High above, Mary could see her friends in the control room: Owen, Robert, Colin, Dr. Cornish. They were all watching her. Then Dr. Cornish held up a jar of peanut butter and licked from a spoon, inquisitively.

(*Pb?*).

Mary nodded in understanding.

She fired the gun.

At first the Starspawn belly laughed, probably at Mary for firing such a small weapon at such a large creature. But then its laughter died and became more of a strange wheezing sound. It dropped Nick to the ground and glanced around, confused.

This is what the Starspawn thought:

What the hell did she shoot me with? The last time I came to this planet there weren't weapons that shot lead over a thousand miles an hour! There were just stupid animals crawling around and throwing their feces on the walls and calling it modern art! How long ago was that? Like twenty years ago?

Just then, Owen's team burst into the room, blasting it with flamethrowers and plasma rifles, both of which had little effect. But it did scare the cultists. They cowered in fear and eventually just gave up, throwing their arms in the air. All of their idols fell and broke on the concrete floor.

Yig-Sothoth looked contemplative, then said to itself in thought-speech: *I think that woman glaring at me has at least fourteen more shots in that gun. Dammit. Well, that decides it! I'm leaving! Screw this planet!*

And with that, Yig-Sothoth slouched over to the wormhole. It stuck its foot inside to test the temperature, then turned around to bid a final goodbye. "Later, bitches," it said.

"Close the portal after it leaves!" Nick yelled to Mary. "Hurry!"

"Where's the switch?"

"Behind the artifact. Just pull out the plug from the wall socket." [vii]

Mary ran behind the portal, but before she could find the power cord, something emerged from the wormhole and grabbed Yig-Sothoth by the shoulder—something just as strange and alien. It pulled the Starspawn backward through the blackness.

Silence.

Everyone waited.

Finally, this new creature reemerged. It was crustacean-looking, with black wings and bulbous eyes. Its round impish body levitated above the floor. Something about its appearance seemed familiar to Mary.

Then it came to her. She remembered the story Phillip had told in the morgue, about the alien spacecraft discovered in the Himalayas, and about a creature called a Mi-Go. She also remembered how this particular creature liked to take specimens for study.

In the Mi-Go's hand, perfectly preserved in a portable cryogenic chamber, was the freshly severed head of Yig-Sothoth, the Starspawn of Cthulhu.

"Nice specimen," it said in perfect English. "I've always wanted a Starspawn for my collection." It looked closer and tapped the glass. "Now, has anyone on this planet seen my brother? He's been missing around these parts for the last couple thousand years..."

The End...?

Stay Tuned...

A local TV crew is invited to Dr. Cornish's lab to document his strange hoarding addiction for a future episode of *Hoarders*. But when a member of the crew goes missing, trouble ensues.

As Mary begins her second day on the job, she is informed about the missing person and must team up with a rogue bounty hunter named Hunter Downs to locate the missing crewmember before it's too late.

What happens next is a harrowing chase through a slow lunch line, a strange exorcism of a possessed oven mitt, a showdown with a genetically modified goat, and a frightful descent into an underground sewer where Dr. Cornish's failed experiments roam freely.

Stay tuned for...
Serious Applicants Only: Day Two!
Coming soon.[viii]

Bonus Story

Exclusive to the paperback version only!
Aren't you lucky?

Some Birds Fly North for Winter

Alex Winter watched the woman he was supposed to call grandma. He watched with plastic binoculars that didn't work too well. The focus knob had grains of sand that snapped between the gears, so it couldn't twist all that far, and everything looked clouded through the lenses. The binoculars were part of a whole NYPD cop set, complete with plastic revolver, gold badge, and handcuffs made of actual metal, key and all.

From his tree fort, he watched his grandma through the window of the upstairs guest room. She rocked back and forth and stabbed her quilt with long knitting needles. Her hands worked far quicker than he would have thought possible for a woman in her eighties. Her hands were large and wrinkled and spotted with rust.

Alex looked at his own hands, young and smooth and with Little Debbie frosting under his fingernails. He had stolen the treat from the cupboard when his mom was vacuuming, then ran up into his fort so he could snack in peace and keep an eye out on things. It wasn't something an officer of the law would do, he realized, so he decided to change the word "steal" to "borrow." It sounded better. Besides, the stakeout was a full-time job. Cops had donuts. He had Little Debbies.

He licked the sugar from his fingers, frosting all warm on his tongue, and thought about abandoning his post to go grab another, but decided against it. He had already borrowed three. His mother might notice an entire box missing. So, he sat and watched his grandma, waiting for her to conduct any malicious activity.

Alex had the gold badge on his shirt pocket and pistol wedged in his belt, loaded with water he had blessed himself from a Bible a mean Christian had given to him outside the mall bookstore. The man had told him he was now old enough to go to Hell, so he was old enough to read this here book. Alex took the book and threw it in his closet, not knowing that come the following summer, he would desperately need it.

He watched her hands move with needle-flash speed, the oxygen mask secured around her face. Usually, she only used it when she went for walks. She must have had problems breathing today. Suddenly, her face twisted all up. Her lips curled back in a snarl, teeth stained yellow from years of black coffee and cigarettes. She ripped off the mask and clutched at her throat, gasping for air.

Alex thought she was having a heart attack. At least he hoped. Then she burst out laughing and slapped her knee and regarded Alex with dead eyes that looked like shark eyes—the way they roll back when they attack. The directness of her stare caused goose bumps to engulf his arms.

They stared at each other for what seemed like an eternity—ocean eyes meeting bleached eyes—until she finally turned away and went back to her knitting. A little smile played at the edges of her mouth.

Alex was holding his breath. He let it out in a loud wheeze, then pulled out his water pistol from his belt. He put his grandmother's withered face into the sights and feigned pulling the trigger.

Accidents happen all the time, he thought. Especially to old people.

#

When Alex found out his grandmother Roberta (or "Bird" as his dad called her) was coming to live with them, he was out of his mind with excitement. He finally had somebody to play with. He decided their first afternoon would consist of a best-out-of-three marathon of checkers and then *Uno* and finally end with a walk around the block while the autumn leaves danced along the streets. The weather was pretty this time of year, and he thought the fresh air would be a nice treat for her. He told his mother his plan, but she made him promise not to bother grandma too much, because she was old and needed plenty of rest. Alex felt a little saddened by this, but gave his promise and ran upstairs to sort through his games anyway, because it never hurt to be prepared.

The last time Alex saw his grandmother was at the Holbrook Nursing Home, over a year ago. She had been there for the past six months. Her sight was diminishing and she couldn't remember Alex's name. She kept calling him Robby. After correcting her a dozen times, he finally threw his hands in the air and collapsed on the floor in defeat. She just wasn't listening. Then his mother took him to the side and told him it was because dad's name was Robert, and grandma called him Robby growing up, and she was just getting a little confused. This upset Alex; he didn't want to see her confused. But he also wanted her to call him by his right name.

Then a year flew by.

During this time, Alex put some length on his bones, was attacked by three squirrels, and began taking medication just to "slow him down a little." The whole time he waited for the impending news about his grandmother. But to everyone's surprise, she got better, and would be coming to stay with them.

Alex helped his mother make up a nice place for his grandmother to stay in upstairs. He was excited for her to visit, even though she was old and couldn't chase him around the yard like a T-Rex. His dad did that. Alex would laugh and fall down and play dead and then get back up and kick him in the shins and climb a tree and lob pinecone grenades down in a furious assault. (Coincidentally, that's also where the squirrel attack started.) But even if his grandmother couldn't chase him around, it would still be great to have her in the house, because she laughed a lot, and liked to cook a lot—even when nobody was hungry.

Then she arrived and stepped out of the taxicab.

For starters, her skin was on all wrong. It hung in clumps like raw cookie dough and looked funny. Over the next week, Alex would determine that when a monster slipped into the body of your grandmother, it should make sure to resemble her at least a little bit. Not like this thing rolling out of the back seat, all blubbery and weird looking.

She glanced over at him sitting on his tree swing and said, "Go tell your father I'm here." It didn't seem strange at the time, until Alex stormed inside the house and told his father the news and trudged back outside (marveling at how a blueberry muffin appeared in his hand) and got a good look at her eyes and noticed they were dead.

He dropped the muffin on the ground.

"Don't drop muffins, Robby," she said. "I never had a muffin growing up in that swamp down south. Now pick that up and help me get my things."

Alex was about to ask her how she knew about the dropped muffin, since she was obviously blind as a bat, but a slight tilting of her head caused him to shut up. She seemed like a dog hearing a noise far off in the distance. Or maybe she was listening for the question he was about to ask. Regardless, he picked up the muffin, put it in his jacket pocket, and helped her with one of her small suitcases. He led her up to her new room.

Once he opened the door, he forgot how scary she was acting and ran into the bedroom and wrenched open all the curtains. He was proud of their renovation—of all the painting and rearranging and all the new pillows. Grandmas liked pillows. The room was nice and cozy and smelled like fresh lilacs and he wanted to hang out in there, too.

"See," he said, motioning to the window. "You can watch the sun rise in the morning!"

"Don't care for sunrises," she said.

"Really?"

"Too warm on my skin. I like when the sun sets, when it gets cold and dark." She took a long tug from her oxygen and stared toward him with white eyes. For some reason she reminded him of the smoking caterpillar from *Alice in Wonderland.*

It wasn't until later that night, slipping into his covers and waiting for sleep to take hold, when he realized his grandmother had never asked for a hug.

#

A week later Alex found his grandmother's teeth. They were just sitting there in a glass of water on the kitchen sink. Now, if she really wanted to fool everyone into thinking she was his real grandma, then she should be careful about where she hid her costume. This was getting silly. He had a brand-new set of vampire teeth for his Halloween costume, and he didn't keep those out in the open. Then he wondered what else was part of her costume. Since his parents were out grocery shopping, it would be the perfect time to find out.

He tiptoed upstairs and listened at her door. Not a sound. Suddenly he tripped and was in her room. He hadn't been inside in over a week. It smelled like musty clothes and old lady perfume. There was another smell, too, a strong chemical smell like when a barbecue catches fire and all the food burns to a crisp. Within moments, he pinpointed the smell to her closet. He creaked open the door and flicked on the drawstring light. Then he gasped at what he saw.

Decapitated heads.

They were molded out of plastic and each held a wig. He never met anyone with a wig collection. It must be the second part of her disguise. Alex had a fake wig for his Dracula costume, an itchy black thing with a V-shaped widow's peak. She must have been doing this for a long time to accumulate so many costumes.

That got him thinking. The final part of his Dracula outfit was a black cloak. That part sealed the deal and struck fear into all those who saw it. He just had to find the final part of her costume, that's all, and then he could expose her as a fake.

He moved aside some of her dresses and came across her knitting supplies next to a metal basket that looked like a cauldron, except it had a plug for an electrical outlet. Her suitcase sat next to it as well, the one he helped carry the day she arrived. He set the case down on the floor and threw open the lid.

Inside was a book called *The Resurrection of the Flesh*. The illustrations were a little weird, with demons and rituals and other spooky things, but overall the book was kind of neat. He wished he had more time to read it. There was also a photo album with pictures dating back to the 1800s, each depicting a woman in her late teens. The last photo was in color and he recognized the woman as his mother.

Next, he handled various glass tubes that seemed like spice bottles. Each one was labeled differently: *Tongue of Bat, Toadstool Spores, Wormwood Resin*.

It was then he realized they weren't spices at all, but spell components! There was no eye of newt though. That was supposed to be like table salt for witches.

The last thing he found was a locket of brown hair next to a pair of scissors. A memory came to him then, from yesterday morning. He was pouring milk into his stupid non-sugar cereal when he heard a loud SNIP and turned to see his grandmother whistling and hiding something behind her back. When he asked what she had there behind her robe, she replied that it was nothing but a little experiment and he shouldn't worry. Then she mumbled something about a change of plans and asked if he could help her program the TV.

Now Alex knew what was going on. His mother was the target for some crazy voodoo witch spell, but now his grandma was coming after him. There was no way she would use him for any spell.

Alex decided to mess with his grandmother.

He took up the scissors and inspected the wigs. Finding a good match, he cut off a chunk and replaced it with the hair his grandmother had snipped off. He was just about to try on a wig that shot in every direction like a confused spider web, when he heard a sound from the upstairs bathroom.

Alex's heart kicked in his chest. He was taking too long. He creaked the closet door shut and began putting everything back the way he had found it. Just as he sealed up her case and tucked it back by her knitting supplies, he heard footsteps sliding across the carpeting outside, followed by his grandmother's familiar wheezing.

"Robby?" she asked. "Are you in here?"

He clicked off the closet light and slid up to the doorway. Through a crack in the door, he could vaguely see her standing in the center of the room. She tilted her head and sniffed the air as if she were a wolf tracking its prey. Then she took another few steps and was at the closet door.

The handle jiggled.

Alex retreated back from the door. He crouched behind her cauldron, which he now realized was the source of the strange odor. Knitting yarn spilled across the floor in dark entrails. Then he was holding one of her throw rugs in front of him like a shield.

The door swung open and light was everywhere. He peeked around the side of the rug and saw his grandmother towering in the doorway.

"Now Robby," she said, "it's not nice to hide on people. Come out and give your grandma a hug."

She had never asked for a hug. Not in the eight days since she arrived. It was just a trick to get him out of hiding and he wouldn't fall for it.

She crouched down low, searching through the dark with her mind powers, hobbling closer and closer in increments and resembling a large inchworm. She came within a foot of him and stretched her neck out and smiled with those yellow teeth, her labored breath reeking like sour milk.

"I found you," she said, and then her hand clamped onto his foot, pulling him out and into the light. He screamed and kicked and fought against it, but she was too strong.

Then Alex's hand gripped something sharp.

A knitting needle.

He lashed out and punctured her hand. The attack

wasn't deep, but she did cry out in surprise and rolled out of the way, dislodging an entire shelf off the wall.

Severed heads rained down everywhere.

Now was his chance. He ran, quickly. But just as he darted past her stubby little witch feet, something hit his eyes, making them itch like mad. He made it halfway across the room before everything began to shift and transform. Straight angles became curved angles and the world breathed as if he swam underwater. He couldn't move a muscle if he tried.

"Eye of newt," his grandmother said. She placed the spell component back in her pocket and loomed over him. "A witch of the dark arts never leaves home without it."

#

"That's not what the picture showed in your book," Alex said, craning his neck to get a glimpse of her invocation circle. His hands and feet were bound with knitting yarn and a gag hung around his neck, now useless. He was still groggy from the powder. A kaleidoscope of colors danced at the corners of his vision, but it was passing quickly.

"Will you be quiet, Robby!" his grandma shouted. She scooped up oil from inside the cauldron and traced along the edges of the circle. "I've done this many times. I know what I'm doing."

"Yeah, but you're not tracing along the lines. You should have done this before you went blind."

"I can see well enough, child. Just so you know, I did this spell exactly one year ago to your grandmother. She was my roommate at that smelly clinic. Unfortunately, she was the only one I could get alone for long enough."

"You switched bodies with my real grandma?" Alex asked.

"Yes."

"Is she still alive?"

"She died shortly after the spell was completed. My body was much younger, but riddled with cancer, and I needed to switch with the utmost of haste." Her eerie laughter filled the room. "Your grandmother suffered greatly in the end, I'm afraid."

Alex's shoulders sagged. He felt a tear run down his cheek. He had only met his grandma a handful of times, considering they lived so far away, but he loved her dearly. "I knew you weren't her," he said after some time. "She was nice and laughed all the time and liked going for walks. Not like you. You're mean and you sit around too much."

"That's all very nice," she said. "Now hush! I need to concentrate. Summoning Malphas is the trickiest part of the invocation. They don't call him The Deceiver for nothing. I must proceed with the utmost of caution."

"Who is Malphas?"

"An ancient demon."

"Why do you have to summon a demon?"

"Because you need to ask permission to use the dark arts."

"Why do you need permission?"

"That's just how it works."

"So, if I wanted a puppy," he contemplated, "I would have to summon Malphas first, and ask him if it's okay."

"No."

"Why not?"

"Because summoning puppies isn't part of the black arts. You have to ask for something you can't normally buy."

"Oh! So, if I wanted a saber-tooth tiger, or a dinosaur egg?"

She rubbed her temples in agony.

"What about good witches?" he asked. "How do they get stuff?"

"I have work to finish, child. Please be quiet."

Alex snapped his mouth shut and concentrated on his daring Houdini escape. It would happen in T-minus two minutes.

After she finished tracing the lines with the oil, she opened the window and chanted in a strange language. The circle began to glow like hot coals. She hobbled back and sat down with a grunt and threw more spell components inside her cauldron, mixing them up good. When everything brewed perfectly, she ladled out the contents into a silver chalice and pushed it out into the center of the circle.

The water in the chalice began to ripple. Chaotic energy surged through the room, like when the air hangs heavy with electricity right before a thunderstorm. Outside, dark clouds slipped across the sky and the sound of a thousand flapping wings rose with the wind.

Who summons me? a voice from the chalice commanded.

"Your faithful servant," she answered. "Elizabeth Anne Colton."

Ah, my little southern belle. What is your wish?

"I wish to transfer bodies with this child, my Lord. I

desire youth again!"

The stars are right. Your faith is true. You may proceed with the ritual.

She lit the locket of Alex's hair with a candle, placed the remains on a small altar. The hair went up in black fumes.

By this time, Alex was folding up his pocket knife and hiding the remains of the rope underneath a nearby chair. He had also switched around three of her spell components. Now he leaned forward and watched everything with huge, bulging eyes.

And then the demon spoke: *Is this a joke, Elizabeth?*

"What do you mean?" she said.

You are using jasmine for a soul transference ritual. Are you planning on seducing this child? That's just wrong.

"Jasmine?" she said, shocked. She picked up her components and smelled them. "How did that happen?"

Do you wish to trade bodies with a human vessel?

"Yes, of course."

From the hair sample you gave, it seems you would rather trade bodies with a horse in Colorado.

She went speechless.

Now was Alex's chance. "And she got the diagram wrong, too. It's supposed to have two dashes in the center, not just one. And it's supposed to have the letter M, for Malphas, not a W. Are there any demon names that start with the letter W?"

No, there are none. Just the name of my butler, Wilhelm. But he is an imp and not too bright. He cannot grant the ability to use the dark arts.

"She didn't do the drawing right at all," Alex said. "Of course, she is pretty old and blind. But still, that's no excuse."

And the demon said: *You're right, kid.*

"Seems like she's trying to trick you," Alex continued. "I wouldn't let her get away with that. She could go tell all her friends and then everyone will make fun of you behind your back."

The sound of a thousand beating wings filled the room.

His fake grandma finally found her voice again. "Please have mercy, my Lord! I can explain everything! This body is old and blind, and Robby here..."

"Alex," he corrected her.

"What?" she asked.

"My name is Alex."

The sound of flapping wings grew even more ominous. Lightning flashed outside.

You have insulted me with your insolence! And that electric cauldron hiding in the corner is just the icing on the cake! Not that there's any cake down here, or anything...

"Please have mercy!" she cried again.

Moments passed. Then the demon spoke: *I shall grant you your wish, Elizabeth.*

She collapsed on the floor. "Thank you! You will not regret this decision!"

Go now! Go to your new body in Boulder, Colorado!

The circle grew brighter and then there was a flash of light. The woman Alex was supposed to call grandma passed out inside the circle and remained motionless for some time. The sound of flapping wings vanished.

Outside, the storm passed.

#

"Is that your grandma?" Mrs. Anderson asked.

Alex stood on his neighbor's front steps. He couldn't speak clearly with the fake vampire teeth wedged in his mouth, so he plucked them out and stuck them in his pocket. "Yeah," he said. "But don't move too quick or anything. She startles easy."

Alex's grandmother stood in the front yard of his neighbor's property. After the incident last month, it took her a long time to figure out how to walk again. Now she was back down on all fours and drinking rainwater from a kiddie pool.

Mrs. Anderson gave a sorrowful look. Then she grabbed two handfuls of candy and placed them in Alex's bag. "Sorry to hear that, dear. A stroke?"

"Nope. She used to be a witch. Now she's a horse."

"No, I mean a *stroke*. Like a small heart attack. Or does she suffer from dementia?"

Alex wasn't quite sure what she meant. He had run into this problem a few times tonight. When he told his neighbors his grandmother was a horse, some of them laughed and watched her pace up and down the sidewalk and handed him a ton of candy. Others gave him a weird look and shut their door. At least his grandmother was nice now.

"Yeah, I guess," he lied. "She used to be an actress. She was in a bunch of plays."

"Oh, that's so sad. Give your family my blessing, Alex. And Happy Halloween!"

"Thanks Mrs. Anderson. Happy Halloween!"

Alex hopped off the steps and helped his grandma up, then led her to the sidewalk.

"I think I should have gone as a cowboy this year," he said, deep in thought. "It makes sense, doesn't it? Oh well, I guess there's always next year."

Alex led her down the street using some carrots. She loved vegetables now. And she was losing a ton of weight from eating so healthy.

They walked toward the next house and he held her hand lovingly and she snorted and went faster.

She loved going for walks now.

(Originally published in Dark Moon Digest, Issue #8.)

Author Bio

Aric Sundquist is an author and editor of speculative fiction. Born and raised in Michigan's Upper Peninsula, he graduated from Northern Michigan University with a Master's Degree in Creative Writing. His stories have appeared in numerous publications, including *Fearful Fathoms Vol. 1*, *The Best of Dark Moon Digest*, *Night Terrors III*, *Evil Jester Digest Vol. 1*, and *Attic Toys*. Being a writer and a musician at heart, he also enjoys board games, guitar, and traveling. He is the owner and editor-in-chief of Dark Peninsula Press, an independent publishing company specializing in genre anthologies. Currently, he lives in Marquette, MI, with his girlfriend, Elsa, and a ferocious beagle named Bruce. Visit his website at: https://aricsundquist.weebly.com/

This space for rent.

Endnotes

[i] (Copyright page) You need a permission slip from the author's mother to quote from this book. This is enforced by the law.

[ii] (Page 19) This is called BioSteel and is 100% true. Go ahead and search the internet for it... I dare you! It is made from the recombinant DNA of a golden orb-weaver spider and a domestic goat.

[iii] (Page 23) In *The Hero's Journey* by Joseph Campbell, a series of events must play out in order to tell an effective story. This doesn't apply to every story, of course, but it does create a very strong foundation for storytelling. Some of those events are...

- *Call to Adventure.* This is where our heroine decides to leave the ordinary world and ventures out into the unknown. In our story, Mary is given the choice to enter the secret laboratory or flee from an ever-increasing wormhole. True to heroic form, she enters the laboratory, successfully responding to the call to adventure.

- *Refusal of the Call.* This is where our heroine refuses to accept their given role, whether out of duty, obligation, or fear. When Mary is given the opportunity to work for HWC, she instantly rejects the job, saying it is "too weird." But when Owen interjects and tells her the benefits, she realizes she can pay off her student debt and so she accepts the job. She is now our *reluctant* heroine.

- *Supernatural aid.* At this point the heroine gains a mentor, aka: Owen. This is also where the mentor presents the hero with talismans to aid in the quest. (Mary receives a genetically modified lab coat, which is a more modern version of a suit of armor.) This is also where she meets her "helpers" on her way to adventure—Colin, Robert, and Nick. Old-school gamers might refer to these characters as "helpful NPCs."

- *Crossing the Threshold.* This is where our heroine leaves the known world and crosses over into dangerous territory. For many protagonists in classic mythology, this journey is a long and arduous road, and fraught with many dangers. For Mary, crossing over is a bit shorter than normal, and weirder... and it leads to Act 2 of the monomyth: *Tests, Allies, and Enemies...*

[iv] (Page 25) Feel free to email Dr. Cornish at this address. He might even send you a chapter of his new work in-progress, *Confessions of an Angry Mad Scientist.*

[v] (page 36) This uncorrected spelling error should have the Latin phrase *[sic]* after it, which means "as it is written." But isn't *[sick]* more appropriate, given the

stomach matter? I mean subject matter. Also, from now on I will always spell "back together" as "backtogether," and "far apart" as "far   apart."

vi (Page 52) Does Yig-Sothoth have asthma? Or does the creature have a severe peanut allergy? This is something scholars and academics will debate for years to come...

vii (Page 65) Instead of chanting to their dark god for the power to shut down the wormhole, the cultists could have easily walked around back and unplugged the power cable. This might be an author oversight, but at this point, does it really matter?

viii (Stay Tuned...) It remains to be seen if the sequel is *coming soon* or merely *gestating slowly*. If you want a sequel to this strange little story, email the author at: aricsundquist@gmail.com and demand action! He will send you a free short story and a picture of his beagle to enjoy while you wait...

www.ingramcontent.com/pod-product-compliance
Lightning Source LLC
Chambersburg PA
CBHW071333130626
46556CB00004B/1888